How
DEVIL'S
CLUB
Came to Be

This is an original story written by Miranda Rose Ḵaagwéil Worl. Though inspired by ancient oral traditions that have been handed down through the generations, it is not a traditional Tlingit story.

How Devil's Club Came to Be

Copyright © 2017 Sealaska Heritage Institute.
All rights reserved.
Designed in the USA.
Printed and bound in Canada by Friesens Corporation.

Sealaska Heritage Institute
105 S. Seward St. Suite 201
Juneau, Alaska 99801
907.463.4844
www.sealaskaheritage.org

MIX
Paper from
responsible sources
FSC® C016245
FSC
www.fsc.org

ISBN: 978-1-946019-14-1
Book design: Nobu Koch

10 9 8 7 6 5 4 3 2

This book was made possible through funds from the US Department of Education Alaska Native Education Program Grant PR# S356A140060 *Raven Reading: A Culturally Responsive Kindergarten Readiness Program*. The contents of this book do not necessarily represent the policy of the DOE, and you should not assume endorsement by the Federal Government.

Baby Raven Reads is an award-winning Sealaska Heritage education program promoting a love of learning through culture and community.

HOW DEVIL'S CLUB CAME TO BE

by Miranda Rose Kaagwéil Worl
illustrated by Michaela Goade

SEALASKA HERITAGE

Raven was walking along the beach and mourning.
Many of the people in his village had fallen ill and
their shaman, the healer, had gone missing. Desperate,
Raven continued along the beach, hoping to find him.

After many hours, Raven suddenly heard a terrible roar.
A shaman he did not recognize ran out of the tree line.
A giant burst through the trees flailing a spikey
wooden club. The giant grabbed the shaman
and dragged him back into the woods.

Troubled, Raven flew back to the
village thinking, "That giant must be
the one who took our shaman!"

When Raven landed, he gathered his people and told them what he had seen and what he planned to do. He would find the giant and defeat him. But just as he was ready to leave, he began to feel sick. Raven had caught the illness.

Many of the boys lined up, eager to take on Raven's task, but Raven denied them all. Instead, he called upon his niece.

Raven's Niece had always done what Raven had asked of her, and was always ready to listen and learn from her uncle. "You must be the one to fight the giant," Raven told her.

With that, he sent his niece to find the giant.

Just as Raven had done, she began to
walk along the beach. The beach grew
steeper and steeper until she found herself
on the top of a cliff overlooking the sea.

She was just about to continue her search
when she heard rustling behind her.
She turned to look.

Raven's Niece found herself looking up at a huge, shadowy figure. It was the giant. He raised his spikey, wooden club.

As it came down,
Raven's Niece dove between the
giant's legs and shot at him with
her bow and arrows. She watched
with satisfaction as the arrows
stuck into his ankles.

But the giant only growled
and pulled them out. He raised
his club and rushed toward her.
With nowhere to go, Raven's
Niece ran back toward the cliff
and leapt off the edge.

She closed her eyes and prepared to hit the water.

After several moments, she realized she was no longer falling. She was in a village that looked very much like her home, except that all around her were tall beings that looked half-bird and half-human.

The leader approached her. "Welcome! We are the Thunderbird People. Tell us, what brings you here?" the clan leader asked.

Raven's Niece told them of the illness in her village and of the giant.

"Ahhh," said the clan leader of the Thunderbirds, "our shaman was also taken by the giant. Since you are on a quest to defeat him we will help you."

He took off his Chilkat robe and draped it around her shoulders. As it touched her, the weight of the robe seemed to disappear, leaving it light as a feather.

Raven's Niece thanked him and said goodbye. She closed her eyes and prepared to return through the sea that separated their worlds.

She waded into the water, and thought of her family who were sick and of the giant still wandering. She waded out until she was fully under water and the world of the Thunderbirds fell silent.

She found herself, once again, falling.

But Raven's Niece did not cry out.

The voice of the Thunderbird clan leader
boomed in her head. She spread her arms
outward, but they were no longer arms.
They were the wings of a giant bird—they
were the wings of a Thunderbird.

She flew to the cliff where the giant still
stood looking for her. She swooped down,
grasped his spikey club with her talons,
and shredded it into pieces.
Then she circled back.

She sunk her talons into the giant,
flew off with him, and dropped
him into the water, far, far away.

From then on she was known as the Girl Who Defeated the Giant. She returned to the cliff and lay down in exhaustion. She realized she had also caught the illness.

Again, the Thunderbird clan leader's voice called out to the Girl, telling her what she must do. In a haze, she got up and began walking into the woods. The Girl found that where the shreds of the giant's club had fallen, spikey wooden plants had grown in their place.

Taking one plant, she cut a piece of the inner bark and began to chew on it. Chewing on the plant gave her the strength to make it back to her village.

The people were weary from the illness, but rejoiced in the Girl's return. They asked many questions. In response, the Girl told them of the Thunderbird People who had helped her. Then she told them how she defeated the giant and survived the illness. The Girl pulled out the spikey wooden plants she had collected.

She explained how the plants gave her strength and healed her. At first, the villagers were wary, but they trusted the Girl, and chewed on the inner bark.

Once they rid the illness from the village, the people learned to respect the powerful plant.

These plants grown from the shredded bits of the giant's club are what we now call *S'axt*, Devil's Club. Since the giant had fought many shaman, his club had absorbed their healing abilities. To this day, Devil's Club, like a shaman, helps heal and protect us.

about Sealaska Heritage Institute

Sealaska Heritage Institute is a regional Native nonprofit 501(c)(3) corporation. Our mission is to perpetuate and enhance Tlingit, Haida, and Tsimshian cultures. Our goal is to promote cultural diversity and cross-cultural understanding.

Sealaska Heritage was founded in 1980 by Sealaska after being conceived by clan leaders, traditional scholars, and Elders at the first Sealaska Elders Conference. During that meeting, the Elders likened Native culture to a blanket. They told the new leaders that their hands were growing weary of holding onto the metaphorical blanket, this "container of wisdom." They said they were transferring this responsibility to Sealaska, the regional Native corporation serving Southeast Alaska. In response, Sealaska founded Sealaska Heritage to operate cultural and educational programs.

about Baby Raven Reads

Sealaska Heritage sponsors *Baby Raven Reads*, an award-winning program that promotes a love of learning through culture and community. The program is for families with Alaska Native children up to age 5. Among other things, events include family nights at the Walter Soboleff Building clan house, Shuká Hít, where families are invited to join us for storytelling, songs, and other cultural activities. Participants also receive free books through the program.

The program is based on ample research that has shown that Alaska Native students do better academically when culturally relevant content is incorporated into learning materials and classes. The books also help educate non-Native families about Alaska Native cultures and languages, place-based storytelling, and traditional oral literature.

In recognition of SHI's success in applying research-validated practices to promote literacy through Baby Raven Reads, the Library of Congress selected the program for its 2017 Best Practice Honoree award, making it one of only 15 programs in the world to receive the honor that year.

Baby Raven Reads was made possible through funds from the US Department of Education Alaska Native Education Program Grant PR# S356A140060 *Raven Reading: A Culturally Responsive Kindergarten Readiness Program* running from 2015-2017.

Miranda Rose Worl, whose Tlingit name is K̲aagwéil, is an Eagle of the Kaagwaantaan Clan, from K̲óok Hít (Box House) in Huna, Alaska, and a Shangukeidí yádi or Child of the Thunderbird Clan. She graduated from Thunder Mountain High School and is currently a junior at Dartmouth College. Miranda wrote this story while she was a freshman in high school.

Michaela Goade is an illustrator and graphic designer currently residing in Juneau, Alaska. Her Tlingit name is Sheit.een and she is from the Raven moiety and Kiks.ádi Clan from Sitka, Alaska. Raised in Juneau, she spent her childhood in the forests and on the beaches of Southeast Alaska and her artistic style is rooted in the depth and beauty of its landscapes. At the heart of her work, whether it's a logo or book illustration project, is a passion for evocative storytelling. After earning her degrees in graphic design and marketing from Fort Lewis College, she worked as a designer and art director in Anchorage, before embarking on her full-time freelance career and returning to Southeast Alaska.